D0442931

The Big Dip

Melanie Jackson

Orca currents

ORCA BOOK PUBLISHERS

To my sister-in-law, Lynne Jackson—MJ

Library and Archives Canada Cataloguing in Publication

Jackson, Melanie, 1956-

The big dip / written by Melanie Jackson.

(Orca currents)

ISBN 978-1-55469-179-1 (bound).--ISBN 978-1-55469-178-4 (pbk.)

I. Title. II. Series: Orca currents

PS8569.A265B53 2009   jC813'.6   C2009-902582-5

Summary: At Vancouver's Pacific National Exhibition, Joe Lumby, track
star extraordinaire, finds himself caught up in a mystery involving the
theft of a gallery treasure.

First published in the United States, 2009
Library of Congress Control Number: 2009927574

Orca Book Publishers gratefully acknowledges the support for its publishing
programs provided by the following agencies: the Government of Canada
through the Book Publishing Industry Development Program and the
Canada Council for the Arts, and the Province of British Columbia
through the BC Arts Council and the Book Publishing Tax Credit.

Cover design by Teresa Bubela
Cover photography by Getty Images

Orca Book Publishers
PO Box 5626, Station B
Victoria, BC Canada
V8R 6S4

Orca Book Publishers
PO Box 468
Custer, WA USA
98240-0468

www.orcabook.com
Printed and bound in Canada.
Printed on 100% PCW recycled paper.
12 11 10 09 • 4 3 2 1

chapter one

It was coming up—the big dip.

The cars rattled to the crest of the rickety roller coaster. Usually Skip and I got the first seat. But tonight a grizzled old man had dodged in ahead of us. As the train creaked higher, the old man twisted around to grin at us. One eyelid, missing its eyeball, was squinted almost shut. With his working eye he studied me.

"I know you. You're that speedy feller, Mojo Lumby!" the old man exclaimed with a loud cackle.

It was true. I'd nailed the regional and the provincial track championships. The *Vancouver Sun* had done a story on me just last week. *Joe Lumby, Age 15: On the Track, Just Call Him Mojo*, the headline said. There had been photos of me zooming around the school field.

The old guy probably recognized me from the photos. "Yeah, well," I shrugged. I hoped he wasn't going to ask me about my times, not with the big dip coming up.

Besides, the name Mojo was a sore point with me. I was fast on my feet, all right. For me, running was everything. I was almost always training or at meets. The downside was, my grades were tanking. While everyone else got to go away for the summer, I was stuck in Vancouver taking a math course. There was no mojo, no luck, about that.

But for now, I didn't care. The train was edging over the crest. It crashed down the big dip.

At fifty years old, the roller coaster at Vancouver's Pacific National Exhibition is the only wooden one left in Canada. It's also one of the few anywhere that just has dinky metal bars. Most roller coasters have shoulder clamps to hold you in. When you drop in this one, you lurch over the metal bars.

Skip and I leaned forward so we could stretch over the bars. In a whirl of blue sky and rushing air, we lunged, our hands reaching to the tracks.

We always did this. It was as if we were the ride, not the riders.

"Stay still, you idiots!" screeched a woman behind us.

We ignored her. There were shrieks of laughter, and somebody popped the tab off a soda can. I thought that was weird—breaking out refreshments as you plunged down the big dip.

In front of us, the old man leaned forward too. I thought it was cool, being that old and still into roller coasters. On the other hand, I hoped the excitement didn't give him a heart attack.

Slam! The train hit the valley. Skip and I sat back and high-fived each other. Nothing beat the big dip.

The train zoomed up the next hill. The PNE coaster is engine-powered only up to the first big dip. After that, it spools around the twists and turns on its own momentum. Roller coaster nuts from all over the world come here to ride the coaster because it's such a museum piece.

I decided that the old guy in front must be one of those nuts. He was still leaning forward, ready to catch the next dip.

I forgot about the old guy as Skip and I lunged again. Whoa! The grounds of the PNE, with their bright rides and concession stands, swirled around us. The merry-go-round was upside down. And there was the Ferris wheel, spinning straight at us...

Seconds later, or so it seemed, the train sputtered to a stop. Skip scrambled onto the platform. He helped out the passenger behind us, a stocky woman with a large boxy purse.

The old guy in the first seat was still leaning forward.

"Hey, buddy," I said. "Ride's over."

He didn't reply—didn't move.

"C'mon, Joe," Skip called from the platform. "Let's get outta here. We need our junk-food ration for the day!"

The old man moaned. Maybe he did have a heart attack, I thought, alarmed.

I touched his shoulder. "Hey, buddy..."

He straightened up, gasping. His lean face was as gray as concrete. He tried to clutch my arms, but he was too weak. His hands slipped to the sides of my jacket and clenched the fabric.

The stocky woman pushed Skip aside. "I'm a nurse," she said. "Let me have a look at him."

Her face shoved up to mine. Her teeth, small and pointy, looked out of place in her large square face.

"I'm a nurse," she repeated.

I started to move out of the way.

But the old man kept clutching my jacket. His lips were twitching. He wanted to speak.

I leaned closer, blocking the stocky woman.

The old man whispered, "A plant...the Margaret rose...Get it to the police..."

He slumped sideways. His single eye stared up at me, unblinking.

And unseeing.

He was dead.

By now the next train had rolled in behind us. An attendant hurried over to see what the delay was. "C'mon," he urged, glancing at the people waiting to get on. "Gotta move!"

Then he saw the old man. "Jeez," the attendant said, turning pale.

"He must've had a heart attack," I said. I was thinking of how the old guy had stretched forward for every dip. I had assumed he was doing it for fun.

The attendant unclipped a cell phone from his belt and started barking into it about an emergency. His voice broke partway through.

The passengers from our train and from the train behind us crowded around. There were some gasps, but nobody said anything. They just stared.

I realized I was still holding the old man's shoulder. I let go.

The sides of his jacket fell back. That's when I saw it.

The small black hole at the back of his neck. Blood spread from it like a red scarf.

"Not a heart attack," I breathed. *"This guy was shot."*

chapter two

That popping sound I'd heard on the roller coaster—it hadn't been someone opening a can. It had been a bullet.

Skip's eyes widened. The terror in them mirrored mine. I could tell he was having the same thought. While we were leaning over the bar, the bullet had skimmed right over our heads.

People around us were screaming. They started running away, shoving at each other in their desperation to get out.

There were all kinds of people, all ages, shapes and sizes, all scared out of their minds.

The stocky woman caught the fear too. Changing her mind about helping the old man, she used her big purse to push people aside. Behind her was a lean guy with a blue and white Vancouver Canadians baseball cap. He said something to the woman and pointed over the crowd. She kept bashing her way through.

"There's a shooter around here," Skip said in my ear. His voice was choked. It was the first time I'd ever heard Skip sound frightened. Usually he was so confident, so sunny. Nothing fazed him.

"Let's get outta here," he urged.

The attendant looked like he wanted to run too. He bit his lower lip. His freckles stood out against his skin like Frisbees.

I didn't want to leave the attendant alone. It didn't seem right.

Skip gripped my elbow. "Have you forgotten, Joe? You're breaking curfew. You're not supposed to be here."

I was supposed to be home studying. I had a math test tomorrow. But my parents were visiting friends in Whistler over the next two days, and my kid sister Ellie was at a sleepover.

Plus, in the morning Skip was heading out with his folks to their cottage in the Okanagan. The PNE would be over when he got back. Tonight had been our last chance to ride the big dip together until next year.

Skip had free passes to the whole fair. We could take all the rides we wanted. His dad was on the PNE board of directors.

So, I'd snuck out.

Skip was going to tutor me when we got back to my place. Skip sailed through math. He sailed through everything. In September, he was going into an advanced class. Regular schoolwork didn't challenge him enough.

Mr. Too-Perfect, I called him sometimes, and he'd laugh. Privately I wasn't sure I was joking. Skip's being a whiz kind of got to me. I had to sweat most of my subjects just to pass.

I should listen to Skip now, I thought. But my eyes were glued to the old man. Why would anyone want to kill a harmless guy like him?

PNE security guards were rushing onto the platform. The attendant started to cry. I wasn't feeling too good myself.

The attendant could only point a shaky hand at the dead man. The guards shoved Skip and me aside.

Sirens sounded—ambulances and police were coming.

Skip dragged me to the exit. He urged, "We gotta get outta here. What happens when the police see you? What if somebody from the newspaper takes your picture? Your dad will know you went to the PNE."

Dad had threatened to pull me out of track if I didn't improve my grades. This summer course is it, he'd said. This is your last chance.

Still, I hesitated. The old man's face swam up before me again. I heard him mumble his last strange words. I told Skip, "The old guy said something about a rose, the Margaret rose. He wanted me to give it to the police."

"What?" Skip said. "The guy was dying, Joe. He wasn't in his right mind. C'mon. Once we're away from here, you can send the cops a *dozen* roses if it makes you feel better."

I didn't think the old man had been talking about bouquets. But there was no time to think. The sirens screamed closer, ripping our eardrums. Feet pounded up the entrance ramp. Police officers ran over to the dead man.

"You can't do anything for him," Skip said.

I nodded numbly. He was right. The old guy was beyond my help. He'd taken the biggest dip of all—the one that you never come up from.

We bolted down the exit ramp.

Skip came home with me and coached me for the test the next day. "C'mon, dude. I know you can concentrate. I've seen you on the racetrack. Your mind is one hundred percent on the finish line."

But Skip didn't know there was a third person sitting at the table—the ghost of the old man. He was clear to me, even if Skip couldn't see him. One minute the old man was grinning at me—the next, he was slumping sideways.

Finally, after wrestling with the math for ages, I started to get it.

"You can do anything if you just concentrate," Skip encouraged. He was so sure I could do it, it kind of infected me. I started believing that, yeah, I *could* pass the math test.

The next morning, the heat wave that the weather people had warned about finally rolled in—just in time for my math exam.

With no air conditioning in the pre-World War II school, the humidity was thick enough to cut through.

The teacher switched off the lights. "At least we can make it shady in here," she said, wiping a tissue across her forehead. "Now, good luck with your exam."

I stared at the first question. The words wriggled in the heat. *If X is...what would Y...*But I thought I could figure it out.

I unstuck my sweaty arm from the page and started my calculations. X equals, Y equals...

X...Y...

Why would somebody want to kill a harmless oldster?

There'd been a story about the shooting in the morning *Sun. Man Shot on Roller Coaster. Ride Closed While Police Investigate.* The story said the man's name was Jake Grissom. It didn't say anything else about him.

There'd been a quote from the police, asking anyone who had been on the ride to contact them.

I thought of the woman sitting behind Skip and me—the stocky woman with the big purse. Had she been in touch with the police? Maybe she told them about the two boys behind the old man. Maybe the police were on the lookout for us.

I pushed these thoughts out of my mind, or at least to one side of it, and kept slaving away in the heat.

When I looked up after the final question, I was the only student left.

The teacher smiled at me. She was holding a battery-powered mini-fan that blew her hair away from her face. "Are you done?"

"Yeah." I handed in the test. "Thanks for waiting," I added. I bet she wanted to escape this hothouse as much as I did.

"It's okay. See you next class, then." The teacher put my test in her briefcase.

She headed out and down the hall.

The outside doors in this school locked behind you, so I could leave on my own. I decided to go splash some water on my face before I left.

I headed to the basement where the restrooms were. It was cool down here, and the lights were off. Only a dim gray light filtered through the frosted windows. The basement felt like a cavern. Every squeak my runners made echoed back, amplified.

Leaning over the sink, I ran the cold water full blast. I peeled off my T-shirt and doused my upper body with water. I washed away the sweat, the Xs and Ys from the test buzzing around in my head, the face of the dying old man...

Nope. Him, I couldn't wash him away.

Should I have stayed till the cops arrived?

What is with this rose?

Good and soaked, I looked in the mirror and pursed my lips into a fish face. I ran my forefinger over them and made loud blubbering noises. They echoed back. Mojo Lumby, the one-man entertainment show.

I didn't bother toweling off, just pulled the T-shirt back over my wet skin. Out in that egg-frying weather, I'd dry off right away.

I walked past some lockers. I knocked on the doors, one after another, to hear the hollow echoes.

The locker at the end of the hall was open. I hadn't noticed that when I came through before.

As I got closer, I reached out to pull the door closed. Then I'd knock on it too. I liked making all these echoes.

Mojo Lumby, the one-man entertain—

The locker door slammed against me, smashing my nose.

Then the door swung back for round two. *Smash*. This time it punched the air clean out of my chest.

I fell sideways. The crash of my body inside the locker created the loudest echo of all.

chapter three

A bulky figure leaned over me. It was one big shadow, like an oversized inkblot.

The shadow hissed, "Okay, Mojo. Talk. Where'd Jake hide the Margaret rose? What did he tell you?"

I opened my mouth to say, *I don't know.* But blood from my nose flowed in, clogging the words.

"You're not cooperating, Mojo." A gloved fist rammed me into the back of the locker.

This was one strong dude. He clamped me by the throat.

Maybe I could distract him before he cut off all my oxygen.

"Here," I choked. I wrenched my wallet out of my pocket. "Take my money. Enjoy."

I threw the wallet. He let go of my throat to catch it. As he stepped back, I saw he was wearing a trenchcoat, with a ski mask pulled over his face.

This was Trenchcoat's lucky day. The wallet held the fifty bucks Mom and Dad gave me to order out for food.

Trenchcoat didn't act like it was his lucky day though. Not even glancing at it, he stuffed the money in his pocket with a curse. Maybe he'd expected more.

Maybe, to show his dissatisfaction, he'd now squeeze the remaining shreds of air from my throat.

No, he won't, I thought. Not till he gets the Margaret rose.

The thought calmed me—somewhat. I stopped gasping for air. I practiced small steady breaths—runner's breaths.

I edged forward and got my head and shoulders out the locker door.

Trenchcoat tossed my wallet to the floor. My bus pass fluttered out with my mom's instructions for taking care of the house. *Don't forget to check the mailbox each day. Always lock the door. Make sure Ellie eats proper meals. Tell her no veggies, no dessert.*

I fixed my eyes on the paper. I knew what it said—but Trenchcoat didn't.

I choked, "What Jake told me...I wrote it down..."

Trenchcoat followed my gaze. He bent to pick up the paper.

My lungs were still raw from having their oxygen cut off, but my arms were okay. The push-ups and weight lifting I did made them strong. I grasped the edges of the locker and pulled myself out.

Trenchcoat looked up from the paper he was unfolding.

I ran.

I heard Trenchcoat puffing and wheezing as he lumbered after me.

The fire exit was the closest way out. I sprinted to it. OPEN ONLY IN AN EMERGENCY was painted on the glass in big red letters.

I'd say this qualified.

I pushed the door open, setting off an alarm that jangled through the building.

I ran outside. It was twenty-eight blocks to my house. I kept running and never once looked back.

One of the reasons I didn't ace schoolwork was that I hated being confined in a classroom. I thought better when I could move around, and thought best when I could run. I could toss off the distractions like unwanted layers of clothes. When I was running, only what mattered stayed with me.

I rounded the corner of Nanaimo and Hastings and cut through Sunrise Park. I wasn't even out of breath. The mountains loomed in the distance, cool and blue.

I had to go to the police, even if they charged me with deserting the scene of a crime. Whoever shot Jake knew who I was. Like Jake, they'd recognized me from the *Vancouver Sun* story.

Whoever shot Jake.

I thought of the people who'd sat behind Skip and me. I hadn't noticed any of them really, except for the woman with the big boxy purse. She could have had a gun in that purse. She could have shot Jake.

On the other hand, the woman had said she was a nurse. She'd tried to help Jake.

What was this plant Jake had mumbled about?

I reached the end of the park. I'd cleared my brain, all right. The problem was, all that was left were questions.

What was this plant?

The words pounded at me in rhythm with my footsteps.

I veered out of the park and cut across the middle of Hastings—through blaring horns and squealing tires—to a gas station. At the payphone I fished in my pocket. Trenchcoat had the fifty bucks, but I still had some change. I punched in Skip's cell number.

"Yeah?" Skip sounded bored, annoyed. I pictured him in the car with his parents, his iPod buds in his ears. Skip didn't like having his tunes interrupted.

His voice warmed on recognizing me. "Yo, Mojo. What's doin'?"

"The Margaret rose," I panted. "Can you google it? I gotta tell the police about it, like the old guy wanted."

Skip caught the urgency in my voice. "Why, what happened?"

I didn't want to go into the Trenchcoat incident. Skip would be all over me with questions, and I didn't have time. Not with Trenchcoat after me.

"Just look up the Margaret rose for me," I pleaded.

Skip's dad had a Blackberry, a fancy one with all the gizmos. He'd promised one to Skip, if Skip kept up his sky-high marks. This kind of cheesed Skip, who didn't like to wait for anything.

"Can't you look it up yourself?" Skip was needling me. I bet he was still annoyed about having his tunes interrupted.

I leaned my forehead against the phone-booth glass. At home we were still on dial-up. It took a long time for the computer to chug onto the Internet—and I didn't *have* a long time.

I replied, forcing my voice to stay even. At the slightest sign of pressure, Skip would clam up. He didn't like being pushed. I said, "No. I mean, yeah, I could look it up. But if you google the Margaret rose for me now, you'll know what it is by the time I get home. By the time I phone you back. Please?"

"Okay, okay." Skip sounded surprised. "Keep your shirt on, buddy."

I replaced the receiver just as Skip was asking his dad for the Blackberry.

Miss Lucy called the doctor,
Miss Lucy called the nurse,
Miss Lucy called the lady
With the alligator purse!

Ellie was doing cartwheels on the front lawn. With every cartwheel, her long red-ribboned braids spun like windmill blades. Even while flipping, my sister wore her neon pink backpack. She and the backpack, filled with dolls, crayons, pretend makeup and other girly stuff, were inseparable.

"Hey," I said, flopping down on the bench by the rosebush. I wiped my face with my T-shirt. "How come you're home? I thought you were gonna be at Sandra's all day."

Ellie just kept chanting. Every time she said "the lady with the alligator purse," I thought of the woman on the roller coaster—the woman who was either a nurse or a murderer.

The chanting was getting to me. Mom told me to be patient with my sister, but to have to put up with her today of all days...

"What happened, you and Sandra have a fight?" I asked.

Startled by my annoyed tone, Ellie flipped to an upright position and stared at me. "Sandra and I never fight," she responded solemnly.

Then she started with the cartwheels again.

"Mumps," said the doctor,

"Measles," said the nurse...

"Aw, cut it out," I said. It bugged me that Ellie had showed up when she wasn't supposed to. Now I had to worry about her.

I couldn't warn Ellie about Trenchcoat because she'd freak.

"Sandra has pinkeye," my sister was explaining. "Her mom said it could be contagious, so I better go home. I knew you'd be here, 'cause your math class was over. But you were late, Joe. How come?" She paused in a handstand. "How *come*, Joe?"

I stood up. "C'mon inside," I ordered. *And I'll lock all the doors and windows,* I added silently.

"Inside? Who wants to go *inside*?"

"Since I'm stuck with you, we're going to spend a nice, sunny summer day indoors," I snapped.

Ellie's eyes filled with tears. I was being mean, but I couldn't help it. And I didn't care.

"Hiccups," said the lady
With the alligator purse.

Ellie was still at it, even inside. Any minute now her cartwheels would bring down one of Mom's china figurines. That Ellie. She knew she wasn't allowed to do her flips in the house.

Upstairs in my room, I shut the door and called Skip.

"Yo, buddy," he said. "Okay. I googled *plant* and *Margaret rose* for you. There's a Margaret rose, all right. Lemme read you one entry. 'It has creamy outer petals, rich purple center ones.' Like, whoop-de-doo. At least, so I *thought*.

"But I kept reading. 'A true Margaret rose is so rare that it's worth *hundreds of thousands*.' "

I let loose a long whistle. "This had to be what the old guy—Jake—was jabbering about. But why would the police want one? If I were them, I'd prefer coffee and donuts."

"Listen and learn, Mojo. I tried the same search words as before, only under Google News. Smart, huh?"

I could just see Skip's self-congratulatory smile. Typical Skip. But then, he *was* smart. "Yeah?" I said. "And?"

"And bingo, buddy. A genuine Margaret rose is on display here in Vancouver, at VanDusen Gardens."

VanDusen is a posh place with lots of flowers. Nice, I guess. It's the type of place mothers like.

"That's gotta be the rose Jake meant," I said. "But I can't take it from VanDusen, even if it *was* Jake's dying wish. The poor old guy," I sighed.

"Whatever." Skip's voice had a shrug in it. He wasn't the most sentimental person. "Hey, so you're at home now, Mojo?"

"Yeah, in my room. I didn't want Ellie to hear. You know what a pest she can be about stuff that's none of her—"

"You should be phoning the cops, Mojo. Not chatting with me about flowers. C'mon, buddy, this is *serious*."

I caught the urgency in his voice. "Okay, okay, I'll call them now."

Skip hung up. He was right, of course. Like always. Mr. Too-Perfect.

I bellowed through the closed door at Ellie to be quiet. Not because I could hear her very well with the door shut, but because I was feeling irritated. Why did Skip always have to be the one to think of what to do? Did I have to be *slow* Joe all the time?

Wishing I was Skip, with his perfect personality, perfect grades and perfect vacation at Lake Okanagan, I called the police. I told the operator about Jake and his weird message, about running away, about the attack at the school.

And about how Trenchcoat, who had my ID, could be after me at this moment.

The operator said they'd treat this as an emergency. The police would come right away.

Please don't let Trenchcoat show up, I thought. Or, if he does, let the cops get here first.

I thought of what Skip had said about how valuable the Margaret rose was.

I whistled again and noticed how the whistle echoed in the silence.

The silence...

I stood up so fast that I knocked my chair backward. In this house, silence was the wrong sound.

I zoomed downstairs.

The front door was open, the lock smashed. By closing my door upstairs, I'd blocked out Ellie's chanting—and the sound of someone breaking in.

The hot still air from outside rushed through the door and pressed in on me, smothering my breath.

"ELLIE!" I yelled.

There was no answer. I heard nothing but the buzzing of bees in the rosebush.

Propped just inside the door was the knapsack that Ellie never went anywhere without.

chapter four

The hall phone rang. It was buried under a stack of Ellie's *Owl* magazines. I unearthed the receiver just as the call clicked into our message machine.

"*Ellie*," I said.

"Wrong-oh, Mojo," hissed a voice. "Not Ellie."

Trenchcoat, I thought.

The voice went on, "Though little Ellie happens to be my guest."

My spine turned to ice. "No," I said. "No!"

There was a rustling sound, and then Ellie's voice drawled over the line. She sounded like she'd just woken up. "Joe?"

"Ellie!" I exclaimed. "Where are you?"

"I'm so tired, Joe," she sighed.

In the distance, sirens wailed. The police were coming.

"Ellie—!"

The hissy voice came back on. "Want to see her again, Joe? Lemme tell you how to arrange that. Bring the Margaret rose behind the roller coaster tonight at closing time. It'll be dark then." The voice chuckled. "Dark as my soul. We'll do a trade—*if* you come on your own. *If* you don't bring the cops or anyone else with you."

"But I—," I started to protest. I stopped myself. *I don't have the rose.* Trenchcoat thought I had the Margaret rose. And that was my only chance to get Ellie back.

I pulled the front door shut. I didn't want Trenchcoat to hear the sirens.

"Okay," I got out, through a throat as dry as gravel. "Behind the roller coaster, at closing time."

"Be there, Joe—or the item I have for trade gets taken off the market... permanently."

Click.

The phone almost slid out of my sweaty hand. Numbly, I put it down. I couldn't think, couldn't breathe. *He had Ellie.*

Ellie, her braids flying with every cartwheel. Ellie, chanting about the lady with the alligator purse. Ellie, my noisy pest of a kid sister.

Ellie was worth more to me than all the stupid Margaret roses on the planet.

I'd been mean to her before she was kidnapped. I'd been a brute, not a brother.

I wiped my eyes with the back of my hand. Then I realized that red lights were flashing through the living-room window.

A police car had pulled up. The lights spun around me, making me dizzy, like I was stuck on a merry-go-round.

No cops, he'd said. If I told anyone, Ellie would be...

I had to get out of there. I had to get to VanDusen, to the Margaret rose.

Money. I needed money for the admission. My wallet was still on the floor at the school.

Mom kept an emergency twenty under the smiling-bear cookie jar in the kitchen. Knocking the bear on his side, I grabbed the twenty.

The police officers were pounding on the front door. I bolted out the back, plowing through the thick blackberry bushes at the end of our yard.

I climbed over the back fence and ran to the street.

I ran without thinking where I was going. I was on automatic pilot. I ended up at one of my haunts, the Britannia Community Centre. Usually I went into the fitness room to work out, but now I needed somewhere to sit and think.

I went into the Britannia Library. Collapsing on a chair, I leaned my head down and clasped my hands over my knees. I breathed deeply, raggedly, not the way my coach had taught me. A woman at one of the computers glanced over curiously.

Clinging to the woman's hand was a little girl, hopping from one foot to the other with impatience.

My eyes swam. I couldn't look at the kid. I thought of how drowsy Ellie had sounded—like she'd been drugged.

Ellie...Little Ellie...

I went over to the drinking fountain and glugged back water. I could get Ellie back, I told myself. I could make this work. Skip had told me I could do anything if I just concentrated.

I sank back onto the chair and shut my eyes, pressing my fingers over them. Against the backs of my lids, Trenchcoat's bulky shaped loomed.

I sat upright, opening my eyes so that the light blocked out the image of

Trenchcoat. Something—an impression, an idea—was knocking at the edges of my brain. Something I'd noticed but hadn't registered. What was it?

Without realizing it, I'd been scowling at the mom and her kid. The mom looked frightened.

I gave her a sheepish grin, but that didn't cut it with her. She was definitely scared. Dragging her kid off to the library counter, she started whispering to one of the clerks.

Huh? What rule had I broken? Couldn't a guy come in and rest for a min—

I looked down and saw scratches, deep jagged scratches, several of them spouting blood.

I'd been in such a hurry I hadn't noticed my skin till now. My hands and arms were covered with angry red souvenirs of the blackberry bushes. I could only imagine what my face looked like. It sure felt sore, now that I was paying attention. No wonder the woman was spooked.

I jumped up to go wash off in the bathroom. I passed the computers, where the woman had been reading something onscreen.

It was the *Vancouver Sun*'s home page. *What's With The PNE?* the main headline blared.

The story described the burst of crimes at the fair. Aside from the roller-coaster shooting, there had been a break-in at the gallery. A lot of valuables were missing. "What's going on?" a PNE-goer was quoted. "The fair used to be so *wholesome*!"

I didn't stick around to read any more of the PNE's problems. I had enough of my own. With suspicious glances at me, the library clerk was already punching in a phone number. A three-digit one. I didn't have to be top-of-the-class to deduce who she was calling. All the while, the woman and the kid stared with wide, frightened eyes.

I beat it out of there. At the drinking fountain outside, I splashed water over my hands, arms and face. Maybe now I didn't look quite so much like an extra from the *Texas Chainsaw Massacre*.

I ran up to Broadway. I didn't have a plan, but I had a mission. I had to get the Margaret rose from VanDusen Gardens. I caught a 99B bus heading west, then grabbed a bus south on Granville.

I could run forever in hot weather but could not sit. On the bus I started pouring off so much sweat that a woman in a business suit took pity on me and passed over a couple of tissues. I wiped them over my face and neck. They were drenched when I was through.

I smiled my thanks at her. I hoped she'd assume my scratches were a new trend in tattoos.

At VanDusen, I hopped out. I handed the cashier the twenty. She took a long time holding it under some kind of lamp. They'd had a problem with people passing counterfeits, she said.

I chewed on my lower lip. There was a long line of tourists behind me, and I could feel their eyes running curiously over my scratches.

Finally the cashier gave me change and let me in. Then—

"Wait," she called.

My heart thudded sickly into my stomach.

"Your guide to the gardens." Her eyes twinkled as she handed me a brochure.

The brochure folded out to a map of VanDusen. A red arrow pointed to the greenhouse displaying the rare Margaret rose. After washing my scratches some more in the bathroom, I joined a long line of elderly people fanning themselves in the heat. As the women fanned, their perfume carried back to me. The scent of perfume, combined with the waves of fragrance coming from the flowerbeds, was almost enough to make me keel over.

A couple with English accents chatted in line ahead of me. The wife was prattling about some friend of theirs. "She was so pretty at her wedding, remember, Hugo? So dewy-eyed!"

"Uh-huh," said Hugo. He lifted his white sunhat to wipe a handkerchief over his forehead.

The line inched forward like a caterpillar with a full stomach. I thought, Will we ever get there? And, What if armed guards are protecting the plant?

"Hardly surprising her marriage didn't work out. She loved someone else," the woman ahead of me said wisely.

"Uh-huh," Hugo commented. He was red with the heat. I hoped *he* didn't keel over.

Feeling my gaze, Hugo turned and grinned. He gestured to his wife. "Gardeners! What a fanatical group. We've come all the way from Victoria, just to see a flower."

"Oh, Hugo," said his wife. Playfully she tapped him with a brochure.

I grinned back at Hugo. He was a nice guy, I figured, bringing his wife here when the heat got to him so much.

We edged into the greenhouse. *Ooos* and *ahhhs* floated around me. The famed Margaret rose, in a curved stone planter, rested on a round table in the center. The rose was roped off, keeping onlookers about three feet away.

There were no guards in sight.

I thought if I leaned over the rope, I could reach the plant and grab it.

"So lovely," cooed Hugo's wife. The rose's creamy outer petals haloed the rich purple, closed petals at the center. "Like a painting, or a piece of porcelain."

"Or like a vanilla-grape ice-cream bar," I said, wisecracking because I was nervous.

Hugo tipped his head back and laughed. His wife didn't know what to say.

They both moved forward. So did I. Now I was right beside the plant. This was my chance. I stretched out my hands.

chapter five

And then...I couldn't do it. I couldn't steal the Margaret rose. I kept thinking of Hugo bringing his wife all the way from Victoria. I thought of all these other oldsters, so happy to be here.

It was like there was a force field around the rose, stopping me from reaching any farther. I pulled back.

Behind me, an old woman whispered, "I've had the same impulse myself. It would be fun to break off a petal, wouldn't it?

But imagine the trouble we'd be in!" She giggled.

I shook my head. I didn't have to imagine trouble. I already had it. I had nothing to give Trenchcoat. I'd blown it.

I wiped sweat off my forehead with the back of my arm.

"You all right, dear?" asked the old lady.

I turned to say, "I'm fine, ma'am"—and saw, over the old lady's snowy white hair, the stocky woman from the roller coaster.

The stocky woman smiled, showing those pointy teeth I'd noticed before. "Hi, Joe," she said. "Remember me?"

"You're the nurse," I said, staring at her. I couldn't believe it. "This is some coincidence, both of us being here."

She smiled wider. "My name's Babs Beesley, Joe. We should talk about last night."

"Sure," I said. "I'd like to know what you saw. Did you talk to the police?"

Babs Beesley glanced down at the old woman, whose eyes had lit with interest at the word *police*. "We'll talk in the gift shop, Joe. Not here."

In the gift shop, people crowded around display cases and shelves. Nobody was leaving the shop, so it was getting more and more crammed. "They need a traffic monitor," someone grumbled. I heard Hugo politely ask someone not to step on his foot.

I squeezed into an alcove called the Children's Corner, with shelves holding coloring books, crayons, beads and tubes of glitter.

Babs Beesley struggled through the crowd behind me. She held her big purse up like a battering ram, forcing people aside. As she got close to me, her pointy-toothed smile spread wide.

I didn't like that smile. It wasn't friendly. It was hungry.

Alligator hungry.

And Ellie's jumping rhyme came back to me.

Call for the doctor, call for the nurse,
Call for the lady with the alligator purse.

Well, this wasn't an alligator purse. More like cheap fake-leather plastic. Still, I studied the purse as Babs Beesley heaved it through the crowd toward me.

I'd thought before that the purse was big enough to hold a gun, that the stocky woman might have shot Jake. But the woman had claimed to be a nurse. She had tried to help Jake.

Tried to help him...*or tried to force dying-breath information out of him?*

"Almost there, Joe," Babs wheezed from behind her purse.

I remembered someone else who wheezed and puffed at physical exertion. Trenchcoat, in the school basement.

Trenchcoat wasn't a guy. Trenchcoat was...Babs Beesley.

"Okay, Joe," Babs panted. "Time for a little chat." She cracked her purse open and plunged her hand in.

The idea I'd put aside jumped back into my brain in grisly Technicolor. Babs Beesley was Jake's murderer. She'd shot Jake with a gun she'd pulled out of her purse.

The gun she was pulling out now...

I grabbed a mega-size tube of gold glitter off the shelf. Peeling off the cap, I squirted it into her tiny black eyes and all over her big, pasty face. She brayed like a mule.

The purse fell, exposing the black gun she clenched. We'd already attracted attention with the glitter. Some had missed Babs and sprayed other people. Now, at the sight of the gun, screams filled the shop.

"Grab the gun," shouted Hugo. He sprang at Babs and started wrestling it away from her.

Babs may have been out of shape, but she was strong. In spite of the glitter I was dousing her with, she kept gripping the gun. Hugo slowly bent her arm backward. Though braying with pain, she didn't release her hold.

Hugo's wife and another woman pushed their way into the Children's Corner. Uncapping more tubes of glitter, they joined me in slathering Babs Beesley. A huge gold pool of it plopped into her open mouth. Choking for air, she finally let the gun go.

Hugo and I forced her to the floor. Hugo sat on her. He beamed at me. "And I thought VanDusen would be boring!"

People crowded around. Two security guards pushed through, ordering everyone to stay calm. They'd called the police, they said.

The police! I couldn't let the police get hold of me.

One of the guards put a hand on my shoulder. "Good work, son, helping to disarm this woman. There could have been a tragedy."

I just nodded. I couldn't say what I was thinking—that there still could be a tragedy. Sure, the stocky woman was out of the picture—but where did that leave Ellie? *Where was she?*

I tried to edge my shoulder free of the guard's hand without seeming too abrupt.

"The cops will want a statement from you," the guard said. He was smiling, but he still held on to my shoulder.

The ear-splitting crackle of a loud-speaker made everyone jump. A crisp voice announced, "Phone call at the entrance for Joe Lumby. Repeat, for Joe Lumby."

"Joe Lumby?" repeated the guard, releasing my shoulder. "Where I have heard that name before?" He crinkled his brow. "Hey, you're *Mojo* Lumby."

Everyone's gaze swiveled to me as I walked to the entrance.

The cashier handed the phone to me under her window.

"Hello?" I said.

I glanced back into the gardens. The two security guards were striding toward me—along with two police officers. The cops must have used a service entrance.

The guards didn't look so friendly now. They had grim "gotcha" expressions.

A voice hissed into my ear. "Very funny with the shenanigans at VanDusen, Joe."

Ellie's kidnapper! Not Trenchcoat, a.k.a. Babs Beesley, after all. Someone else.

Someone who was here, watching.

"Yeah, funny, ha ha," I gabbled, buying time. "Mojo, the one-man entertainment show, that's me."

I craned around, surveying the gardens, the entrance, Granville Street. Where was he?

"Cut the cackle, Joe. You want your sister back, or what?"

"Yeah, I do. I'll have the rose for you, I promise. Uh..." My gaze panned the street again, past a man talking on a cell phone—

And swung back to the man. He wore a Vancouver Canadians baseball cap.

It was the lean man from the roller coaster. He'd run away with Babs. He was her accomplice—and Ellie's kidnapper.

He was talking to me on the phone right now.

I turned away, in case Baseball Cap looked at me. He looked leaner and meaner than I remembered. I didn't want him to know I'd spotted him. Now I had an advantage. I knew what Ellie's kidnapper looked like, but he didn't know I knew.

I blathered, making my voice uncertain, as if I had trouble remembering, "Behind the roller coaster at closing time, right?"

He gave a scornful chuckle. "Bravo, Joe. By the light of the...*shivery* moon, shall we say?" The voice grew grim. "And remember: no rose, no kid sister."

Click.

chapter six

The guards and the police were almost on me. The sun glinted on the handcuffs dangling from one officer's belt.

I shoved the phone back under the cashier's window. I glanced out at the street. Baseball Cap had left—unaware that I'd seen him.

Ducking under the turnstile, I barreled through a line of people waiting to get in. I felt like a bowling ball crashing into pins.

One lady in high heels lost her balance and toppled backward.

I was sorry about that, but there was nothing I could do. I couldn't risk getting nabbed by the cops. I had to make that meeting tonight. I didn't have the Margaret rose, but maybe I could bluff Baseball Cap.

I broke into a run. The guards and police started running too. I heard them pounding behind me. But I didn't worry about them. I could outrun anyone.

I have to make that meeting. I have to get Ellie back.

I jumped on the first bus heading back up Granville and switched to the Hastings bus. I couldn't go home; the police would be watching for me. So, I headed to the PNE. I'd wait out the hours till closing time.

And try to think of a way to bluff Baseball Cap.

The Hastings bus was packed with kids heading to the PNE. The windows were cranked open as far as they would go. Big difference that made. The bus was a steam bath.

A girl from a couple of my classes got on the bus. She was a friend of Skip's more than mine. I'd had the impression she liked him—but then all the girls liked Skip. He always knew the clever thing to say to them.

I unstuck myself from my seat and stood up so she could have it. She smiled and said hi, but I just shrugged back at her. I didn't want to talk.

I moved to the back of the bus to make way for other people getting on. Gripping the overhead rail, I pressed my forehead against my arm and shut my eyes. Me, bluff Baseball Cap, I thought. Right. I'm fast on the feet, not on the wits.

I thought of what Skip had said. *C'mon, dude. You can do anything if you concentrate.*

I had to do it. I had to get the better of Baseball Cap somehow.

I took a deep breath, opened my eyes—and looked straight into the face of a policewoman.

Wait. She was wearing a uniform, but she wasn't police. She was a transit official.

All the same, her stony gaze locked on me. "What's the matter with you, kid? What are all those scratches? *You been in a fight?*"

My lips were dry. I ran my tongue over them, but it was dry too.

"We don't want trouble," the transit woman said. "Not in this heat. Maybe you should get off the bus." She fingered a cell phone sticking out a side pocket of her purse.

"No trouble, ma'am." I forced the words out of my parched mouth. "That's not it. I..."

People were watching us. Among them, the girl from school.

I said, "My girlfriend's up there. She wants me to go join her. Excuse me, ma'am."

I pushed past everyone. They all just kept gawking.

The girl's name was Amy...Amy Claridge, that was it. She had long dark hair and stared at me solemnly. She was wearing a red smock with a design of orange flames on the front. Above the flames, black letters proclaimed HERBIE'S RED HOTS. Herbie's was a food stall at the PNE, famous for its extra-spicy hot dogs.

I stared back at her as sweat dripped down the side of my face. I wasn't like Skip. I had nothing clever to say.

So, leaning down, I just whispered, "Please. Don't give me away."

Her dark eyes were doubtful. I didn't blame her. I looked like a cat's scratching post, not a law-abiding average Joe.

Around us people started talking again. The transit official took an empty seat and looked out the window. Little kids squealed with the excitement of going to the PNE. Nobody was listening to me.

I said, "Please trust me, Amy. I can't have that transit lady reporting me. I'm in trouble. My kid sister's life is..." Is at stake, I was going to say, but it sounded too corny for belief. Instead I just shook my head. The whole thing *should* have been beyond belief. Except that it was real, it was happening. It was a nightmare that plowed on and on and wouldn't stop.

My face must have reflected my misery, because Amy said in alarm, "It's okay, Joe. I–I won't say anything."

I managed a crooked grin of thanks. She sure had dark eyes—like lake water at midnight. When she smiled, lights appeared in them.

I wondered what there'd been between her and Skip. They'd hung out together a lot those last couple of weeks at school.

As if reading my thoughts, Amy said, "I guess Skip's left for the Okanagan. I was hoping he'd call me first, but..."

She likes him, all right, I thought. I wiped my forehead with the back of my arm. "Yeah, so?" I said, kind of rudely. It was always Skip with girls.

Amy's cheeks turned pink. "I wanted to talk to him. About an essay."

"You brainiacs," I said. "Guess you like to stick together, huh? Compare A's?"

She looked down at the purse in her lap.

"I'm sorry," I said. "I'm just kind of preoccupied. So...you work at Herbie's. What's that like?"

"In this weather? Hot and smelly."

I laughed. There was a plastic container attached to the bus wall, with pamphlets about bus routes and stuff. I took one out, waved it a few times and gave it to her.

"Here," I said. "Instant fan."

I walked Amy toward Herbie's Red Hots. It was past the roller coaster, near the Farm Country building, with sheep, cows and other animals of the Old MacDonald variety. The occasional *moo* and *baa* floated out. They reminded me of Babs Beesley and the braying sound she'd made.

And of her buddy, the guy with the baseball cap. I clenched my fists in my pockets.

I'd told Amy about Babs. I'd told her about Ellie getting kidnapped and Baseball Cap demanding the Margaret rose as ransom.

I hadn't shared the where and when of the exchange though. I didn't want Amy to turn noble and insist on coming along. I had to do this on my own.

Across from Herbie's was the Community Police Center, a small white clapboard building. I stopped. "Maybe I better leave you here," I said.

Amy nodded. Frowning, she fiddled with the strap of her purse. Then she blurted, "That old guy who was shot—Jake something..."

"Jake Grissom."

"Yeah. Well, the other day I saw him with someone. A friend, I think, because they were talking really intently."

A policewoman came out of the Community Police Center and surveyed the fairgrounds. She was just catching a few rays, maybe...or maybe not.

I took Amy's elbow and guided her around another building, the Horror House of Mirrors. There was a long lineup. We swerved to the other side of the line, out of the policewoman's view.

"Jake's friend," I said. "Was it a stocky woman? Or a guy wearing a baseball cap?"

"No," said Amy, her dark eyes troubled. "Nobody like that. It was *her*."

And she pointed past the Horror House of Mirrors lineup—to the policewoman.

The Horror House of Mirrors line shifted past us. To avoid standing out, Amy and I joined the end of the line. Screams, creepy organ music and villainous laughs blasted out at us.

According to the Horror House sign, once you got inside, you'd be too confused to escape. You'd be creeped out and disoriented by the strobe lights, mirrors and sound effects. Not to mention the cold water and fake spiders that got tossed at you.

The policewoman, still surveying the fairgrounds, pulled out a cell phone and started gabbing into it. Maybe someone had reported seeing me, and she was keeping a lookout. Maybe, maybe, maybe.

I turned my back to her. I said to Amy, "If Jake was talking to the police, he could've been snitching on his buddies."

"His buddies...Babs and the guy with the baseball cap," Amy whispered back, nodding. "What you're saying is, they killed Jake to silence him."

"And all over a plant." I told her about the Margaret rose.

"Unbelievable," Amy commented. "I have a cousin who's fanatical about stamps, but *flowers*...?"

She checked her watch. "I gotta get to work, Joe." Her eyes fixed on my face anxiously. "I don't like to leave you."

I thought how nice she was. Skip was a fool not to call her. If a girl like that liked me...

But she didn't. "I'll be okay," I told her. "Thanks for your concern, but just forget about all this. It's not your problem."

We'd reached the entrance to the Horror House of Mirrors. Amy hesitated, uncertain. Without saying any more, I paid the attendant and pushed through. Amy turned and walked slowly away.

Good one, Joe. Trample on the girl's feelings. I felt rotten. I was tempted to chase after Amy and apologize.

There was a tap on my shoulder. "Amy," I said in relief and spun round.

But it wasn't Amy.

It was the guy in the baseball cap.

chapter seven

Baseball Cap shot out a hand to clamp my wrist. A smile flickered over his lips. The smile scared me more than his lean mean expression had.

But I had the advantage of knowing who he was. I dodged behind a tall statue of a screaming woman. I didn't think Baseball Cap would want to attract attention by knocking the statue down to reach me.

In a breath heavy with the stench of cigarettes, he said, "Just thought we should check in with each other, Joe. About the Margaret rose."

"Boo-waaahhh-ha-ha!" squealed the canned laughter from the Horror House.

"With your personality, you must feel right at home here," I told Baseball Cap. "And yeah, we understand each other. You bring Ellie, I bring the rose."

"You got the rose now?" He stuck his face close to mine. His breath could've been used as a fumigator.

Ahead of us, attendants opened double doors. White strobe lights poured out. One lit up Baseball Cap's face, accentuating his close-set eyes and his thin lips pulled over his yellow teeth in that smile.

"C'mon in, everyone," boomed a deep voice. "If you dare...Boo-waaahhh-ha-ha!"

I shoved the statue at Baseball Cap. He staggered back a few steps, the painted woman in his arms as if they were dancing.

Throwing the statue down, he reached into his breast pocket. That side of his jacket stuck out more than the other side. Which meant...

Another villain, another gun. This was getting all too familiar, like a rerun of a TV show that had been a stinker to start with.

A horde of noisy kids shoved their way in, carrying us forward in a giant wave. I yelled at Baseball Cap, "You get the rose when I get Ellie, not before!"

I shoved people aside and barreled into the Horror House of Mirrors.

The strobe lights spun around me, flashing on for a second, then off. On, then off. The effect was blinding, worse than darkness. I smashed into a woman holding a little girl's hand. When the lights flashed on, I saw the woman's and the girl's faces reflected in about twenty different mirrors. The woman opened her mouth wide for a good laugh-filled scream.

I pushed past her—and rammed into a mirror. Now I got the concept. In the Horror House of Mirrors, you didn't know what was a passageway and what was the *reflection* of a passageway. Fun.

The canned laugh burst out yet again. "Boo-waaahhh-ha-ha! Watch for surprises!"

Water doused me and the other people crammed in the narrow crooked passageway.

Then there were the surprises that weren't on the menu. Baseball Cap loomed near me several times over. "Out of the way," he barked at the kids.

Wrong group to order around. "No, YOU git outta the way, mister!" Moving as a pack, they rammed into Baseball Cap— sending him *thwack* into a mirror. The crackle of falling shards mixed nicely with the canned screams.

As Baseball Cap fell, his gun toppled out of his pocket. Now the screams around me were real.

"Carrie Sue!" shrieked the woman next to me. She hoisted her kid, and, trying to flee, promptly bumped into another mirror.

Carrie Sue started bawling. I thought of Ellie, being who-knew-where and scared.

I put my arm around the woman's shoulders. "It's okay," I said. "Stay close. I'll get you and Carrie Sue outta here."

Sight was a useless sense in this place. It was better to rely on touch. Still holding onto the woman, I started feeling my way out. Whenever I didn't touch glass, I knew I was making progress.

"It's okay, Carrie Sue," the woman soothed her daughter. "This nice boy is helping us. Oh, thank goodness," the woman breathed, as we glimpsed blue sky at the end of the last passageway. "Daylight! What a relief!"

I was glad to see daylight too. I'd had enough of the Horror House of Mirrors to last a lifetime.

On the other hand, daylight might make my own lifetime a short one. In daylight, I'd be an easy target for Baseball Cap.

"Horrible!" Carrie Sue's mom exclaimed to the attendants and people in line. "Guns...broken glass..."

"Cool!" breathed several kids. A boy my age gloated, "I *knew* the Horror House of Mirrors would be the best ride ever."

I was about to take off when the woman grabbed my arm. "And this wonderful boy got us out of there. What a hero! You deserve an award, son. I'm going to phone the police chief about you *right now.*"

She fixed plier-like fingers on my arm. Her eyes were moist with gratitude.

"Uh...please don't bother," I said. My gaze kept veering to the dark interior of the Horror House.

Then, what I'd been afraid of happened. Baseball Cap stumbled out of the Horror House exit—holding his gun.

I pulled my arm free.

Carrie Sue's mom screamed.

She stared at her hand, which had come away bloody. I looked down at my arm. Blood poured from a deep cut near my elbow. I'd scraped it on a broken mirror shard without even realizing it. It was like the blackberry bushes all over again. In my panic, I hadn't felt a thing.

Everyone was gawking at me.

Their stares were like a radar signal to Baseball Cap. Following them, he homed in on me. His eyes met mine.

Then somebody shouted, "He has a gun! *He has a gun!*"

People panicked. They collided with each other in an effort to get away from Baseball Cap. Then, like a massive paint spill, they spread all over the fairgrounds.

I ran with them. Being part of a mob was solid cover.

It didn't last long though. People scattered in different directions.

I had to go somewhere too. But where? The PNE exits were too far—Baseball Cap would see me.

My desperate gaze panned the fairgrounds. Colors, smells, blue sky and sun melted together.

Then a smell scorched my nostrils.

Red hots on the grill.

chapter eight

Amy cleaned my injured arm with rubbing alcohol from the Herbie's first-aid kit. The sting distracted me from what was happening over at the Horror House. A police officer was stringing yellow caution tape in front of the entrance. Others were pacing around, jabbering into cell phones.

I knew they were talking about the gun-toting man. But I didn't want him to be found. I needed to meet him later so I could get Ellie back.

Amy murmured, "Poor Joe. It's like you're up against Hydra."

I didn't know what she meant by Hydra. Skip, I thought sourly, would.

I said, "Lemme guess. Hydra power— the new feminist electricity."

She laughed. "Hydra was a monster in Greek mythology. Cutting off its head didn't work, because it sprouted new ones. What I meant was, just when you get rid of one enemy—Babs Beesley—you face another one."

A cunning one too, I thought. Baseball Cap had kidnapped my sister without making a sound.

He was slippery as those oily red peppers gleaming on the Herbie's grill.

And I had to outwit him tonight.

I wrenched my mind away from my worries and looked at Amy. Again I noticed how dark her eyes were. Dark and deep and sympathetic.

"Here's what I don't get," I said. "Baseball Cap phones me and makes a deal to swap the Margaret rose for Ellie.

After that, Beesley follows me to VanDusen and pulls a gun. What's the point in her doing that? If she shoots me, how do they get their plant?"

Amy shrugged. "Maybe they thought they could fast-track the process by getting the rose at VanDusen." She chewed her lip. "Except...you didn't have it yet. You hadn't removed it from the display."

We stared at each other. Both of us shook our heads. "Doesn't make sense," I said slowly.

We were sitting on footstools, so the Herbie's counter hid us from passersby. I heard a familiar "Carrie Sue!" and stood up to make sure the lady and her kid were okay. I felt responsible for wrecking their afternoon. It was my fault that Baseball Cap had barged in and smashed up mirrors.

Mom and kid seemed to be over their Horror House experience. They were beside a vendor wagon loaded with mountains of candy floss. Carrie Sue had dropped a huge blue-floss-filled cone on the ground.

"Oh, Carrie *Sue*," her mother was scolding. She dug in her purse for money to buy another cone.

"Blue candy floss," grimaced Amy. "How can Katie Sue eat that?"

"Carrie Sue," I corrected.

And I thought: Carrie...*Sue*.

Then I knew what I'd got wrong.

Clutching my forehead, I slumped back onto the footstool. "*Carrie Sue*. A double-barreled name."

Amy plunked back down beside me. "Yeah, so?"

I was so stunned that I could barely reply. "Margaret Rose isn't a flower, Amy. *It's a person.*"

Across from Herbie's, workmen carried a huge mirror into the Horror House to replace the one Baseball Cap had smashed. A cop stood by the caution tape, preventing anyone else from going in. His face grew redder and redder in the hot sun.

Amy took a jumbo Coke over to him, courtesy of Herbie's. It was a nice gesture— and it gave her the chance to ask if they'd caught the man with the gun. I saw the officer shrug. Then, no doubt to impress Amy, he scowled around the fairgrounds. I scooted away from the counter and sat down in front of a computer.

It was several minutes before Amy got back. I teased, "What was with the long chat? Seems to me our boy in blue over there has a thing for deep dark eyes."

She blushed. "He's just lonely, Joe. He has to stand there for the hour, at least. I felt sorry for him."

I thought again how nice Amy was. I said, "If you ever get tired of Skip, let me know, okay? It may be tough to believe now, but my life is generally crime-free. Reassuringly dull, even."

Amy smiled. "Thanks, Joe. It's just that Skip and I...Well, I know he's away right now, but when he gets back..." She stopped, embarrassed.

"Yeah, I understand," I said. I cleared my throat. "Uh...I think I've embarrassed us enough for now, so let me deftly change the subject. I just googled *Margaret Rose*,

only this time without the word *plant.*
Get a load of this."

I turned the screen toward her.

Amy's mouth formed an O.

Another dark-eyed, dark-haired beauty
gazed back at Amy from the screen. This
one had something Amy didn't, though.

A crown.

I said, "Amy, meet Margaret Rose.
Princess Margaret Rose of Britain."

We read about the princess. Younger
sister of Queen Elizabeth II, Margaret Rose
had died in 2002. "Being a heavy smoker
contributed to the princess's early death,"
the biography concluded.

I drummed my fingers on the side of
the keyboard. Too bad about the Princess's
lifestyle choices, but what concerned
me was her connection with Jake. "Jake
referred to *the* Margaret Rose," I said. "As
in, something named after the princess?"

"It has to be something to do with
her," Amy said. She moved the keyboard
in front of her. "Let's try typing *The
Margaret Rose.*"

Entries leaped up. *The Margaret Rose, considered the gem of Scottish culture...*

"A jewel," exclaimed Amy.

"Makes more sense than a plant," I said.

Our hopes lasted the full two-and-a-half seconds it took to load the site. Three red-haired women in frilly blouses and kilts beamed at us from onscreen. A fiddle version of "My Bonnie Lies Over the Ocean" blared out the computer speakers.

"'The Margaret Rose, named after Britain's beloved late princess, is a talented trio of fiddlers,'" Amy read aloud in a flat voice.

"'Book these lovely lassies for your wedding,'" I continued. I covered my face with my hands and groaned. "I'll be booking them for my funeral."

chapter nine

There were millions of Margaret Rose entries. We started clicking through them. It was like searching the Pacific for a lost toothbrush. There were Margaret Rose boats, tearooms, china patterns. There was even a Margaret Rose muffin plate.

There was nothing that thieves would be desperate to get hold of. Nothing that I could give to the police.

Then the Herbie's computer froze. I guess it was feeling as discouraged as we were.

While Amy rebooted the computer, a couple of boys approached the stand. They were both chubby and chewing bubblegum.

"Herbie's is closed due to an E. coli outbreak," I informed the boys.

"Huh? Whaddya mean?"

"Ma gave us money for red hots. We want red hots!"

"Get lost," I ordered.

The boys walked slowly away, glaring back and muttering. I was pretty sure the words they were muttering would not have warmed Ma's heart.

Amy was thinking about other words. "We're not getting anywhere with *Margaret Rose*," she pointed out, twisting a strand of her hair. "Maybe we should think about what else Jake said. He mentioned a plant."

"Yeah?" I scowled at the two chubby boys, who were still glaring at me. "So, okay, *plant*. I'm thinking leaves, stems, little bumblebees."

Amy ignored my bitter humor. "I saw Jake talking to the police, right? That makes me think of another kind of plant. A *police plant*, as in police informant."

I was impressed. "If Jake was a plant, that could be why Babs Beesley shot him. He was snitching on her and Baseball Cap. Give this girl a gold medal—or the collected DVDs of *CSI*."

Amy grinned. "Now if we could just figure out *what* Jake was snitching about."

The computer was ready again. Newly inspired, I started up the Internet.

But before I could type anything, the two boys stormed back. A security guard marched right behind them.

"What's this about an E. coli outbreak?" the guard demanded. "Why is Herbie's still open? Why haven't I heard about this?"

"There's no E. coli outbreak at Herbie's," Amy told the guard.

Shoving his bubblegum into a cheek, one of the boys blurted out, "Yeah, well, *he* told us we couldn't have red hots."

The kid pointed at me in the back. I shrugged and pretended to concentrate on the computer.

"There is no E. coli outbreak at Herbie's," Amy repeated coldly. "I'm sorry to hear such rumors being spread."

Good girl, I applauded silently. The best defense is an outraged offense.

The guard swung his annoyed gaze to the two brothers. "What are you guys doin'? Creatin' trouble?"

Out of sheer nervousness, I was having trouble not laughing. If I laughed, the guard would get mad. He'd be on me like an ant on a picnic cake.

I distracted myself by reading. The home page was the *Vancouver Sun* news site. I read the story that the woman at the library had been reading. The story about the crime wave at the PNE—the gallery thefts and the shooting.

On the other side of the counter, one boy whined, "We don't lie, do we, Bruce?"

"Not often," his brother replied. They both sniggered.

I read about the missing valuables that had been on loan from the Royal Museum

in London. For security reasons, the story
didn't specify the items stolen.

I swerved my eyes back. The *Royal*
Museum. In *London.*

"That guy on the computer. He started
it!" one of the boys shouted. The other one
swore, colorfully as a rainbow.

"Uh, buddy—can I ask you a few
questions?" the security guard demanded.

They were talking about me, to me,
but I couldn't take my eyes off the story.
The type blurred, swam together. Again
I remembered Jake whispering to me.
I remembered him clutching my jacket.

On a hunch, I did a quick Google search.

And then I knew, I *knew,* what the
Margaret Rose was, and where to find it.

But there was no time now. I had to
concentrate on getting Ellie back.

There was a new voice on the other side
of the counter.

"What's the problem here, Amy? These
folks bothering you?" The policeman had
come to investigate.

"N-no. No bother," Amy said nervously. She didn't look at me. "I'm going to make red hots for these two nice boys. On the house."

The boys sniggered again. They were getting rewarded for whining. Amy had probably ruined them for life.

"Sounds good," the policeman said, frowning. "We don't want any trouble."

Then the policeman gave Amy a look.

An understanding look—followed by the faintest of nods.

It hit me.

The cop knows. Amy told him. That's why she had talked to him for so long.

Amy started cooking a couple of red hots. The policeman nudged the guard and the two of them walked away. The boys smirked.

I stepped casually into the storage room. Pushing open the back door, I ran.

chapter ten

Fireworks blazed over English Bay. High in the night sky, they formed a silver globe. The globe hovered, glittery and bright. Then it dissolved into fading streamers that disappeared into the water.

Most fairgoers had left to watch the fireworks from a better viewpoint. PNE staff were dimming the fairground lights. Compared to the sky, the fairgrounds were dark, almost inky.

Like Baseball Cap had whispered to me on the phone: *It'll be dark by then. Dark as my soul.*

I edged out from behind a kiosk plastered with ads. I peeled off an ad and wiped sweat off my forehead.

It was closing time. I watched the roller-coaster attendants walk toward the gates.

I'd wait a few more minutes and then go behind the roller coaster as Baseball Cap had instructed.

I thought about Amy. By now she'd have closed down Herbie's and gone home. I should have known I couldn't trust her. I couldn't trust anyone. I was on my own.

Amy was a nice girl, but she didn't get it. She didn't understand that I couldn't risk bringing the police in. She'd only pretended to agree with me on that.

If Baseball Cap suspected the police knew, he might not show tonight. I might never get Ellie back.

At the thought, my throat went dry. *Don't panic*, I told myself. Panic is no good.

I shut my eyes, felt the cool night air on my skin and took some deep breaths.

I couldn't be mad at Amy. She'd meant well. Skip was lucky to have her waiting for him. If I made it through this, I'd tell him so.

Hiding behind the kiosk, I counted my blessings, few as they were. I hadn't told Amy where I was meeting Baseball Cap. I hadn't told her what and where the Margaret Rose was.

I thought about Baseball Cap's phone call. His threats were carved on my brain. But I still felt I was missing something. It loitered at the edge of my mind.

A movement caught my attention. A figure at the now-shadowy entrance was heading toward the roller coaster.

Baseball Cap?

Dragon-red fireworks blitzed the sky, making the fairgrounds even murkier. I had to squint to follow the figure. When it reached the roller coaster, it faded, shadow into shadow.

I didn't think the figure had been wearing a cap. Also, it looked bulky, not lean.

Staying close to the shadows of the rides, I edged toward the roller coaster. I walked slowly around the coaster. I'd never been there when it was shut down. It loomed in the dark, bony and rickety, like a dinosaur skeleton.

All was shadows, stillness and silence.

A door opened, spilling out a cone of light. A figure stepped in front of the light so that it was just a silhouette.

This wasn't the bulky figure I'd seen running toward the coaster. I was sure of that. This person was lean. This must be Baseball Cap, without the baseball cap.

But who was the bulky guy? And where was he now?

Behind Baseball Cap, I saw a panel of switches and a large lever—the control booth.

Baseball Cap was still a silhouette, but there was something weird about his head. It was all smooth.

He had a nylon over his head, I realized, to disguise himself.

He hissed, "So? Where's the Margaret Rose?"

"Where's Ellie?" I demanded.

Baseball Cap pointed to the first car on the track. I could just make out a slumped form inside. "What have you done to her?"

He whispered, "Shhh, Mojo. Don't want to attract attention, do we? She's sleeping, with a little help from me. Not to worry, it's just sleeping pills."

I started toward her.

"Not so fast, Mojo." Baseball Cap reached a hand back to clamp the lever.

The nylon twisted his face into a leer. Or maybe he *was* leering. There was a note of pleasure in his whispery voice. He was enjoying himself, the sicko.

"One wrong move," he said, "and little Ellie gets the big dip—without a safety bar. You can imagine what would happen then, huh, Joe? The car drops and Ellie goes flying."

He clenched the lever. I was hypnotized by the sight. I couldn't pull my eyes away.

I said dully, "I don't have the Margaret Rose with me. But I know where it is. I can tell you, if you'll just let Ellie—"

"Not good enough, Joe." Baseball Cap

stepped back into the control booth. In the light, his nylon-distorted face was grotesque.

Realizing I was staring at him, Baseball Cap muttered a curse, and switched off the control booth light. "The Margaret Rose, Joe."

He glanced over at Ellie.

He flexed his fingers on the lever.

What to do? I couldn't bluff. He knew I didn't have the Margaret Rose—

Wait. Rewind. He'd said, *So? Where's the Margaret Rose?*

How did he know I didn't have it?

If he knew about the Margaret Rose, he would know how easy it would be to carry.

Something didn't compute here. If this guy had been involved in the gallery break-in, he ought to be familiar with the Margaret Rose.

I needed to buy time. I needed to think.

I held my hands up. "Okay, okay, you win. I stashed the Margaret Rose nearby. I'll get it for you."

Maybe he wasn't working with Babs Beesley, after all. That would explain why Babs had come after me. *She hadn't known about Baseball Cap kidnapping Ellie.*

But Baseball Cap had been at the roller coaster when Babs had shot Jake. They'd fled together. That couldn't be coincidence.

If it wasn't coincidence, what was it?

"Hand it over now, Joe," snarled the figure in the control booth. "Or Ellie wings it to the stars."

I glanced at my sleeping sister. She looked so little. My eyes stung. I couldn't think anymore. I was petrified with fear for Ellie.

But something knocked at my brain. It hovered just out of reach.

Words. That's what the something was. The kidnapper's words on the phone.

It'll be dark then. Dark as my soul.

*By the light of the...*shivery *moon, shall we say?*

And just now:

Hand it over now, Joe. Or Ellie wings it to the stars.

That wasn't thug talk. It was clever talk.

I stared at the figure in the control booth. Rage and realization filled me with the hot urge to kill. No wonder Ellie had been grabbed so easily from my house. *She'd opened the door.*

I lunged forward and tackled Skip, throwing him to the ground.

chapter eleven

I kneed Skip in the throat. He was choking as I tore the nylon off his head.

"You were supposed to be in the Okanagan," I shouted, shaking him. The back of his head crashed against the pavement. I wanted to kill him.

I glanced at Ellie again. She was safe. And I knew I wouldn't kill Skip. I wouldn't give Ellie a murderer for a brother.

Skip coughed. His voice came out ragged, frightened, un-Skip-like. "Please understand, Joe. I wouldn't have hurt Ellie. I just wanted to cut loose, y'know?"

I shifted my knee back from his throat. I held him down, but I didn't bash him around anymore. "No, I *don't* know. You tell me."

Skip's voice gained strength. "Last night I heard Dad telling Mom about the gallery thefts. He said something about the Margaret Rose, and I remembered what Jake gasped out to you. I wasn't sure what the rose was, but I knew it had to be worth a bundle."

I didn't think it was possible to loathe anyone as much as I did Skip at that moment. "Go on," I said.

Skip's voice grew almost cheerful. He was so sure that good old, not-too-bright Joe would forgive him. Skip could clever-talk his way out of anything.

He said, "I thought, what if *I* could get hold of the Margaret Rose? I wasn't sure how I'd manage it, but I knew I didn't want to go to the Okanagan. I told Dad and Mom that I wanted to sign up for an advanced-math

summer course. They went for that, easy—
they love it when I show initiative. They're
always saying I'm too lazy."

Skip chuckled. "If they only knew! The
deal was, my aunt would come to stay with
me. But as soon as Mom and Dad drove
off, I told Auntie I was visiting you for a
few days. She didn't need to come till later
in the week.

"When you phoned, I pretended to be
heading to the Okanagan. But all the time
I was at home, right across the street.

"After our conversation, the old brain
kicked in. If I pretended to kidnap Ellie,
you'd tear the planet apart to find a Margaret
Rose. Like I always tell you, Mojo, you've
got this intense ability to concentrate, even
if you don't realize it."

Skip grinned—and even now, hating him,
I felt the old infectious encouragement.
The guy had charisma. That's what made
him so dangerous.

I clenched my teeth. "Talk."

Skip explained, "When I knew you'd be
busy talking to the cops, I slipped across

the street. I tapped quietly on your front door and told Ellie to go over to my house right away. We were going to plan a surprise party for you, I said. She skipped ahead like an excited puppy. The kid loves me, Joe."

"All the girls do," I said bitterly.

"Then I twisted your front lock off with a screwdriver so you'd think a stranger had forced his way in.

"At my place, Ellie started to whine about her dumb backpack, so I gave her hot chocolate laced with Mom's sleeping pills.

"Know how I got Ellie here?" Skip's tone was warm, confident. "I drove her in Mom's car, the one we keep the wheelchair in for my gran. Once I parked, I simply wheeled Ellie into the fairgrounds."

Skip paused. I think he was waiting for congratulations on his brilliance.

Good thing he couldn't see my face. I wanted more information from him. "Who were the other guys?" I demanded. "The guy with the baseball cap, and the bulky guy I saw a while ago."

"Never saw any baseball-capped guy." Then Skip chuckled. "But the bulky guy is one of the attendants. I paid him to unlock the control booth after everyone left. I pretended I wanted a free ride. Instead, he got a free crack on the skull. He's over there"—Skip jerked his head toward the trees—"sleeping it off."

"I saw Baseball Cap by VanDusen Gardens," I said. "I thought he paged me. But it was you."

"You bet." I could hear the smugness in Skip's voice. "I followed you to VanDusen."

I could have pointed out that Skip wasn't as brilliant as he thought. He'd been thinking of the wrong Margaret Rose all along. But I felt very, very tired. I didn't know what to do. I couldn't hold Skip down for hours on end, and I couldn't pummel him into unconsciousness either—tempting as that was.

He was weak. He wouldn't have any fight left in him. I figured I could let Skip up while still holding on to him.

Then something totally unexpected happened.

Skip's grin wavered. His face crumpled. Tears poured down his cheeks.

This, from Skip—confident, nothing-fazed-him *Skip*?

Shocked, I released him. He sat up. The tears flowed on. They had a more powerful impact than if he'd punched me.

"I'm so sorry," Skip wept. "So sorry, Mojo. I screwed up big-time. I went too far. I wouldn't have hurt Ellie. You're my best friend. You know I wouldn't hurt your sister."

Maybe I knew that. Or maybe I didn't know Skip at all.

"I'm gonna let you go for now," I said. "I want you to get outta here. Away from Ellie and me. I'll decide what to do about you later."

I stood up. He struggled to his feet, swayed and staggered off.

I rushed over to Ellie. She was slumped against the safety bar. Jumping into the car, I put my arms around her. "Wake up, El." I stroked her face. "You gotta wake up."

She moaned.

With a sudden lurch, the train was in motion. Light flooded out of the control booth. Skip grinned at me.

He'd pulled the lever.

The train clattered along the rails. If I was alone, I could have jumped free—but not with Ellie.

"Sorry, Joe," Skip laughed—a crazed, gleeful laugh. "I couldn't let you tell anyone. Think about it. There's *no way* I could let you spoil my life."

"SHUT IT OFF, SKIP," I yelled.

Still laughing, Skip shook his head. "I always *could* get the better of you."

The train started its climb up to the top of the big dip.

I hauled Ellie off the safety bar, then yanked it up. If I could just pull the bar down over us...

It was too late. The train had reached the peak.

It crashed down the big dip, pitching Ellie and me forward, out of the car. I clung to the bar, stopping us from hurtling off.

I braced my feet on the floor and jammed a hip into the side of the car to weigh us down.

The rails flew past. Below I saw Skip laughing. My hand, clutching the bar, was stiff with pain.

The icy air whipping into our faces woke Ellie. Not knowing where she was, she screamed and tried to shove me away.

My hand slipped from the bar. My feet left the car floor. We slid over the front edge. The black wind, spinning up echoes of Skip's crazed, dark-soul laughter, sucked us forward.

chapter twelve

Then, with a jolt, the train hit the bottom of the big dip. As it climbed the next hill, we smashed back onto the floor of the car. The safety bar slammed against my skull.

Ellie screamed and punched me. She still didn't know who I was.

We kept climbing. Ahead of us, gold fireworks torched the sky. Their strands seemed to urge us to plunge toward them.

I was dizzy, and for an instant I thought I was in a race. I thought that I'd run my heart and lungs out and couldn't go any farther. I stared at the fireworks. They were saying, *Why struggle? You'll never make it anyway. Give up. Relax...*

But I couldn't give up, not till the finish line flashed below me. I was a runner, not a quitter.

I hoisted Ellie up as far as I could. I was able to bring the safety bar down under her chin. It was the best I could do. If Ellie didn't choke to death, she'd have great horror stories for her grandchildren.

We reached the peak and crashed down. I gripped the sides of the car and pressed my weight against the safety bar. I couldn't be sure I'd secured it.

"Joe!?" shrieked Ellie, scrunched up beside me. "Where are we? What are you *doing*?"

The train plunged to the next valley. She screamed.

"Think of it as tough love," I yelled.

I'd been on this coaster a million times. I figured we had seven, eight, more dips ahead of us. The good thing was, none of them was like the big dip.

The bad thing was my head was ringing, and I was getting confused about what was up and what was down. My hands were ice blocks. The wind seared into my skin. I felt like I was going to pass out.

The fireworks were now white-hot and blinding. They filled the fairgrounds with light.

Skip was yelling. He hadn't given up. When the train slid up beside the platform, he would be waiting.

One last dip and the train slowed to a glide, smooth as a swan on a lake. In a second it would stop.

I was battered and sick. My mind wandered in and out of racetrack hallucinations. And now I'd have to take on Skip again.

I squeezed my eyelids shut to make the dizziness go away.

The train stopped. A hand closed over mine.

Fists clenched, I pulled away from it and forced myself to stand. "I'll kill you," I told Skip.

I tried to swing a punch. Instead, I swayed.

Nothing happened. No one punched back.

I blinked hard against the blinding white lights. There was a face in front of mine, but it wasn't Skip's.

"I'd prefer not to be killed, if you don't mind," said Baseball Cap.

Amy had been right. Bad guys popped up like Hydra heads.

I swung my fist back. I'd hammer Baseball Cap, all right. I'd hammer them all. Bring 'em on.

Baseball Cap raised a hand to ward me off. With his other hand he calmly tossed a coin up and down.

I couldn't hit him because now there were two Baseball Caps, two coins going up and down. I was hallucinating again.

I stared hard at Baseball Cap, willing him to come into focus. I thought of how he'd shadowed me to VanDusen. How he'd grabbed my wrist at the Horror House.

People talk about puzzle pieces falling

into place. In this case, it was more like a piece being taken away. I'd assumed Baseball Cap was a thief and a kidnapper. I saw now that I'd been wrong.

I lowered my fist. Baseball Cap reached out, took hold of my elbow and steadied me.

"Thanks, officer," I said.

Baseball Cap, known better as Vancouver Police Detective Mike Gagel, had already called a couple of ambulances. They waited, red lights flashing, behind the searchlights the police had targeted on the roller coaster.

I saw a smaller flashing red light in the distance. It was the police car that was taking Skip to the station.

Before switching on the searchlights, the cops had crept up on Skip and pounced. That's why Skip had been yelling, Detective Gagel explained.

As I thought, Amy had told the police everything. At least, everything she knew.

"Lucky for you, we got a warrant to search your house," the detective told me. "That's how we found out about your meeting tonight. Skip's instructions were still on the answering machine."

I remembered grabbing the phone just as the machine clicked on. Thank god for Ellie dumping her *Owl* magazines on top of the phone.

Thank god for Ellie being safe. I heaved a huge ragged sigh. As far as I was concerned, she could chant about alligator purses 24/7 if she wanted to.

I couldn't speak for a moment. Detective Gagel tossed a coin up and down, pretending not to notice that I was teary-eyed. He was lean but maybe not so mean, I decided.

"I don't *want* to go to the hospital," my sister wailed. Pulling away from an ambulance attendant, she ran up and threw her arms around me. She was half scared, half excited. "What's going on, Joe? How come we were on the roller coaster? I wanted to go to Skip's party. Skip *said* I could."

Then Ellie rocked her head in her hands and moaned. "I dunno why I have such a headache, Joe. And my stomach feels queasy. Maybe it was something I ate."

"Maybe it was something you drank," I said. I grinned at the ambulance attendant, who was looking warily at my sister. I guessed he didn't spend too much time around female eight-year-olds. *Yakkety-yakkety-yak.*

"You need to go to the hospital," I told Ellie. Remembering how mean I'd been earlier, I lifted her and gave her a hug that made her squeal. Then, gently, I unfastened her arms from around me. "We both need a trip to the hospital. I'll join you soon. First I gotta talk to the nice detective."

Ellie wrinkled up her nose at Detective Gagel. "Mister, your breath would clobber an *army*."

"Yeah, yeah." The detective flipped his coin some more. "So I forget my Tic Tacs occasionally. We all have bad days."

I would have grinned, but that would have made my skull ache even worse.

chapter thirteen

Ellie trotted off, still jabbering, to the ambulance. Detective Gagel spun the coin. "I understand you and your friend figured out that Jake was a police plant."

Your friend. *Amy*. Was she here? I squinted past the searchlights.

It was more likely she'd followed Skip to the police station. It was Skip she'd be worried about.

Detective Gagel explained, "Jake Grissom was working undercover to catch Babs

Beesley, who specialized in robbing galleries and museums. Jake convinced Babs he could fence the loot from the PNE gallery.

"He told Babs he'd get millions for the Margaret Rose. Babs handed it over—but then she had second thoughts. Maybe someone tipped her off. We'll never know.

"Jake and I were meeting here to return the Margaret Rose to the gallery. Jake arrived ahead of me. The roller coaster was his favorite ride. He must've decided he had time for a spin on it.

"He didn't realize that Babs was following him. "When I arrived on the platform, I saw her hunch down behind you and Skip."

Detective Gagel stopped tossing the coin. He clenched it till his knuckles turned white. "I blame myself for not putting a tail on Jake. If only I'd protected him..."

"You did your best, sir." Now I knew Detective Gagel hadn't been running with Babs. He'd been running after her.

He managed a smile. "And you did *your* best, son. In fact, you did better.

You caught Babs Beesley for us. When VanDusen security phoned, I rushed over. But by the time I got there, you'd scrammed."

I said ruefully, "I saw you talking on the phone. I thought you were Ellie's kidnapper. It took me a while to figure out what the Margaret Rose was." I shook my head. "At first I thought it was a flower. Then I realized it couldn't be.

"So I thought back to after Jake was shot. He pretended to be holding onto my jacket—*but he was really dropping the Margaret Rose into my pocket.*"

"Which is where we found it," Detective Gagel said, "when we searched your house."

He flipped the coin up one last time. Then he held it out to me.

And there she was, the late Princess Margaret Rose of Britain, captured in profile on a solid gold coin.

"Dated 1952," said Detective Gagel, holding the coin so I could read the print. *Her Royal Highness Margaret Rose, younger daughter of King George VI.* "What makes the coin so valuable is that only a few were minted.

The King died that year, so the coin was immediately out of date."

"She sure was pretty," I said, studying the young princess's profile. "Kind of sad-looking. Maybe she didn't like being a princess."

"Not an easy job," agreed Detective Gagel. "Why, I recall my mother telling me that Princess Margaret Rose couldn't even marry the guy she wanted to."

I remembered VanDusen Gardens, and Hugo's wife gossiping about somebody's unhappy marriage. I thought she'd been talking about a friend.

Then I forgot about princesses. Amy walked up to us. She smiled shyly.

I wanted to smile back, but decided not to risk a worse skull ache.

"I hope you don't mind that I talked to the police," she said.

For a long moment I just looked at her. "*I* hope I'm not hallucinating again," I said at last. "That you're here, I mean. I thought you'd be...I mean, what with Skip..."

"I wanted to tell you about Skip," she blurted. "About why I had to see him. I was afraid you'd be angry, though, being his best friend."

The detective lifted his eyebrows. "Catch you later, Mojo." He sauntered off.

"Huh?" I said to Amy. "I guess my brain is powering down faster than I thought. Do you mind explaining?"

She hesitated, then said in a rush, "Skip plagiarized an essay of mine. I thought he should admit it and redo his essay. We had a big argument about it.

"That's why I wanted to see him," she finished. "I'd decided to report him if he didn't admit it himself. I wanted to give him one last chance."

"And you thought I'd be upset at you?"

"Sure." Amy gazed at me, her dark eyes worried.

I knew I'd be upset at *Skip* for a long time, maybe my whole life. I'd liked him. I'd trusted him. And he'd betrayed me.

But I wasn't upset at Amy. I'd tell her that.

First, however, I just grinned at her. Let the skull ache.

Melanie Jackson is the author of the popular
Dinah Galloway Mystery series. *The Big Dip*
is her first entry in the Orca Currents series.
A creative-writing mentor for the Vancouver
School Board, Melanie lives in Vancouver,
British Columbia.